it's only arnold

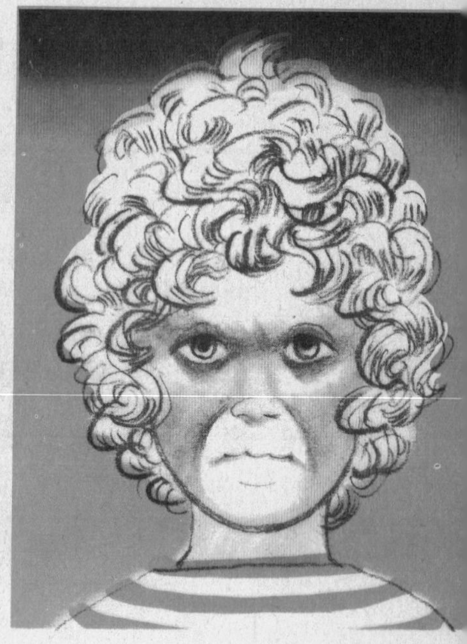

Brinton Turkle

it's only arnold

The Viking Press
New York

Viking Seafarer edition issued in 1975 by The Viking Press, Inc.,
625 Madison Avenue, New York, N.Y. 10022.
Distributed in Canada by The Macmillan Company of Canada Limited.
Library of Congress catalog card number: 73–5139
Printed in U.S.A.
1 2 3 4 5 79 78 77 76 75
Pic Bk
SBN 670–05096–2

for Chris Kelly

On a visit to his grandmother's house, Arnold was helping clean out the attic.

"That," said Grandma, "is your Uncle Robert's old make-up kit." She was holding open a battered suitcase full of tubes and jars and cans and brushes and pencils.

"What does he do with it?" asked Arnold.

"When he used to act in plays, he'd make himself up so you'd never know who it was," Grandma said. "I might as well throw this stuff out. He'll never use it again."

"Can I have it?" Arnold asked quickly.

"Well," said Grandma after a moment, "I guess so. But I don't want my house cluttered up with this stuff. Take it out to the garage and play with it."

Sylvia and Tommy, Grandma's next-door neighbors, and Jasper, Mike, and Peggy from down the street stared in amazement at Arnold's treasure.

"It's paint for actors' faces," Arnold explained. "Do you know how to use it, Sylvia?"

Sylvia was an artist and she was the oldest. “No,” she said. “But I can find out. There’s a book about it in the library.”

There were three books about theatrical make-up in the library. Sylvia read them all, and on Wednesday afternoon she was ready. Since the make-up belonged to Arnold, he was the one she experimented on.

"Make me look like a monster," Arnold said.

Sylvia mixed the colors. She smoothed and patted them onto Arnold's face. With brushes she made shadows. With pencils she made lines. After he was powdered, she handed him a mirror.

"Wow!" said Arnold. A horrible monster looked back at him. "How do I get this off?"

"That's easy," Sylvia said. "Cold cream."

"I'm going to scare Charlie," said the monster.

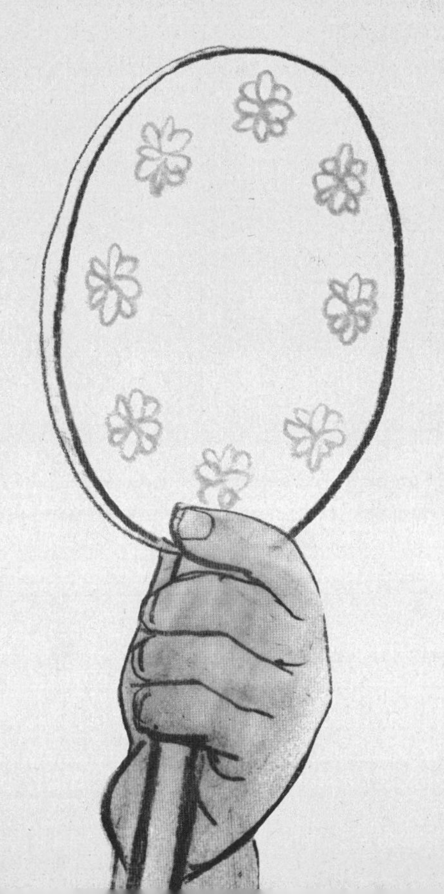

Grandma's big brown dog Charlie was taking his afternoon nap on the front porch.

"Be careful," said Tommy. "He won't know who you are and he might bite."

"Charlie's never bitten anybody in his life," said the monster. "He'll be so scared he'll run and hide."

They all watched from behind a peony bush while the monster crept up onto Grandma's porch.

"*A A A A A G H!*" it roared.

Charlie opened his eyes and began wagging his tail. Then he got up and gave the monster a big slobbery kiss.

"He must have smelled you," said Peggy. "With dogs it's more how you smell than how you look."

"I want to take this stuff off," said the monster in disgust.

Jasper said, "You weren't wearing the right clothes. Monsters don't wear jeans."

Sylvia smeared cold cream on the monster's face and wiped it off with tissues.

Arnold was glad to have his old face back again.

The next day, an old black raincoat hanging up on Grandma's back porch gave Arnold an idea. He grabbed it and ran over to Sylvia's house with it.

"Make me up again. More horrible," he said. "This time I'm going to wear this!" And he flapped the black coat in the air like giant bat wings.

This time he was much scarier. When he put on the old raincoat, they all said he was the scariest thing anyone had ever seen.

Mike said, “Are you going to try to scare Charlie again?”

“No,” said the monster with an evil laugh. “I’m going to scare Mr. Todd!”

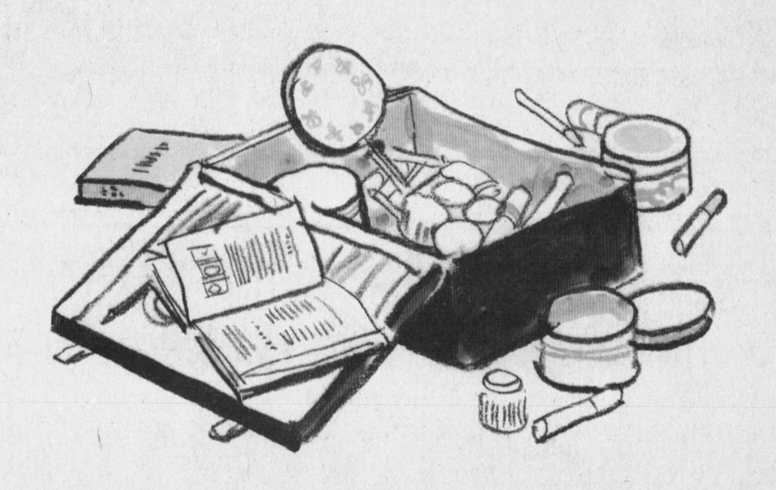

Mr. Todd lived in the big yellow house on the other side of Grandma's. He was digging in his garden when the monster approached. It stood behind him, breathing hard.

"That you, dear?" said Mr. Todd without looking up. (He thought it was his wife.)

The monster breathed harder. It groaned just a little bit.

Finally, Mr. Todd turned around.

"Arnold!" said Mr. Todd with a big smile. "What are you all painted up for? Is it Halloween?"

The monster ran back to the garage.

Jasper said, "You should have made more noise. You should have let out a blood-curdling scream."

"No," said Arnold sadly, as his own face appeared again. "I just wasn't meant to be a monster."

The next day Sylvia showed Arnold a magazine. "It's the claws and fangs," she said, pointing to a picture of a movie monster. "All monsters have claws and fangs."

"Well, for Pete's sake," said Arnold. "How am I ever going to get claws and fangs?"

"I can make them for you by tomorrow," said Sylvia.

Sylvia cut out plastic claws and fastened them to an old pair of her mother's gloves. She also made sharp-pointed cardboard teeth.

After a long, long time Arnold was transformed. When the claws and fangs were in place, the effect was absolutely terrifying.

Peggy backed away. "Who are you going to scare this time?" she asked timidly.

"Grandma!" growled the monster, almost losing its fangs.

Grandma was using the vacuum cleaner in her bedroom when the monster stole up the back stairs. She poked the machine back and forth under the high, old-fashioned bed,

while the monster stood in the half-open door and watched patiently. Sooner or later, Grandma would turn around. Sooner or later, she would see it.

At last Grandma turned toward the door. "For heaven's sake, Arnold! What are you trying to look like?" she said. "If you want to come shopping with me, you'll have to get cleaned up."

The monster ran off.

"And put my coat back on the porch," Grandma called after it.

"I give up," said Arnold as he removed his claws and fangs. "Everyone knows it's just me. I can't scare anybody."

"You scared me," said Tommy.

"That's because you're not even six," Arnold said.

When the make-up was all off, Mike and Peggy asked Arnold to come over to their house to see their new kittens. Halfway there, he said, "I think I'll come over and see the kittens tomorrow." Then he turned around and went back to Grandma's house.

On the front porch he gave sleepy Charlie a couple of pats and went into the house.

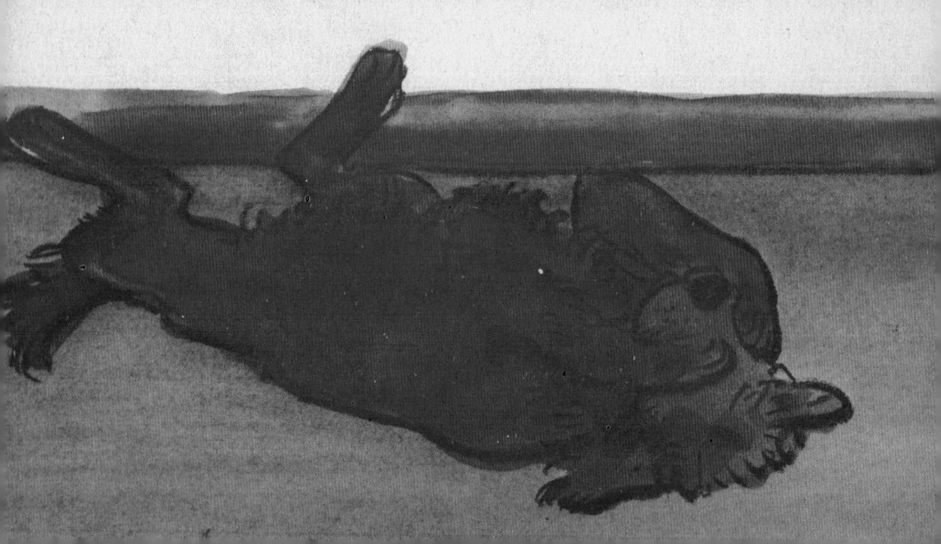

1464

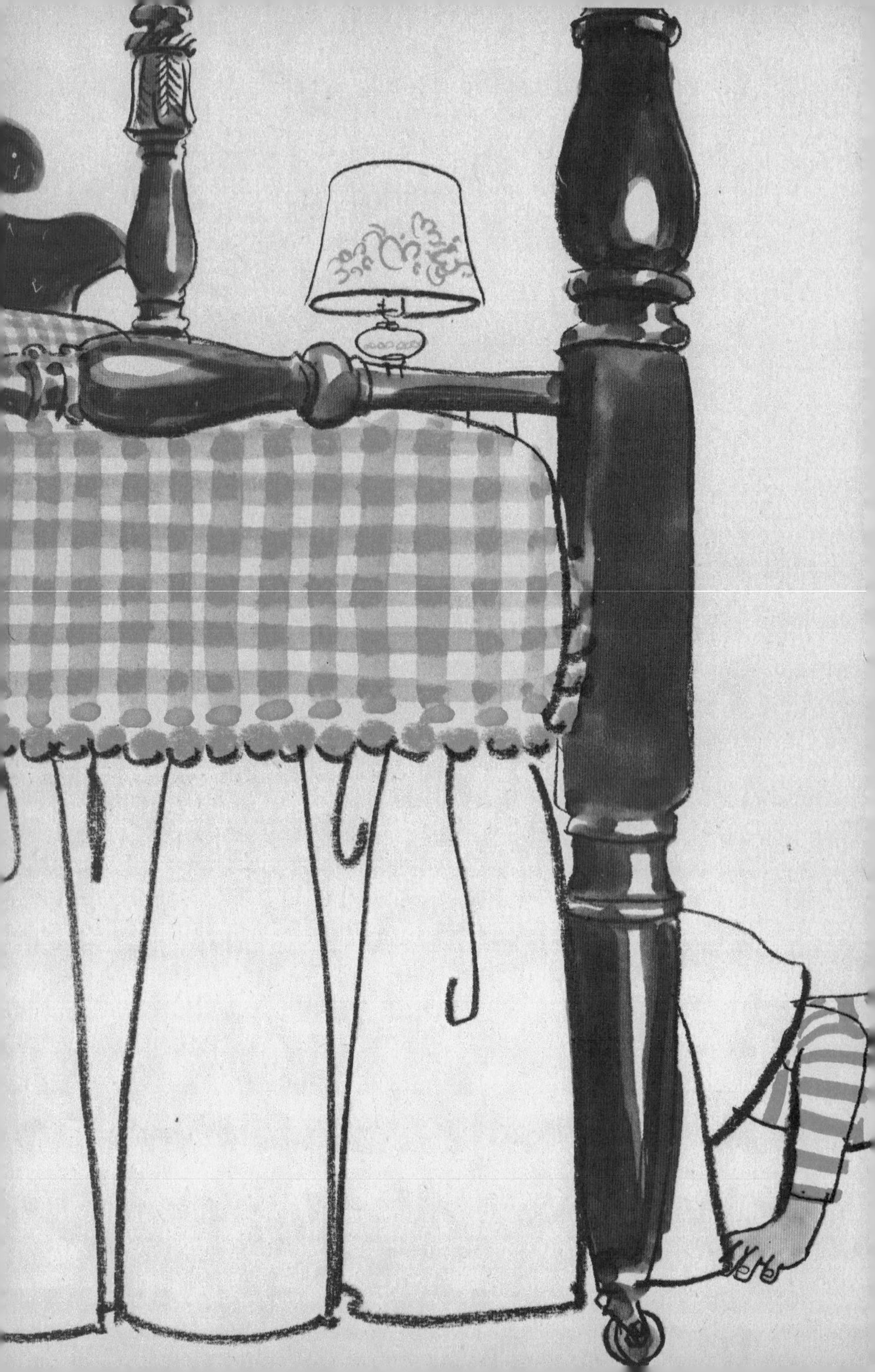

He didn't see Grandma, but he heard her humming in the kitchen.

Slowly, he climbed the front stairs to Grandma's room and crawled under the bed. It was like a tent under there, and it was his favorite place to hide when he wanted to be lonesome and sad.

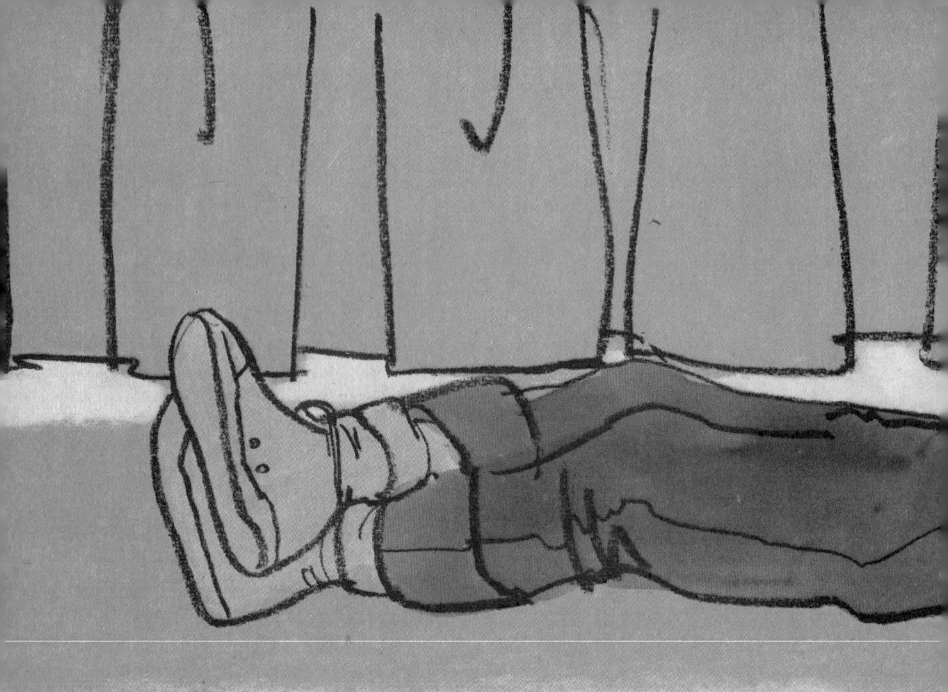

He listened to cars going by on the street and bugs in the trees. He heard Mr. Todd snipping the lilac bushes. He also heard Grandma calling from the kitchen window. “Sylvia, have you seen Arnold?”

“Not for about an hour. He went over to Mike and Peggy’s.”

“I’ll stop by their house and pick him up.”

If there was one thing Arnold didn’t want to do, it was to go shopping.

Soon he heard footsteps on the stairs.

Grandma came into the bedroom. Arnold watched her feet as she walked about the room—to the closet—to the dressing table. He heard her pulling out drawers, closing them, humming to herself.

Arnold didn't move. He didn't want his secret hiding place discovered.

Grandma snapped open her purse. Something dropped to the floor. It was a quarter, and it rolled right under the bed where Arnold was hiding.

Grandma reached under the bedspread. Arnold twisted out of the way, but he wasn't quick enough. Grandma touched Arnold's head. Instantly she pulled her hand back and let out a scream like a fire-engine's siren.

Well, his hiding place was no longer a secret.

Charlie started barking on the front porch.

Arnold rolled out from under the bed. "It's just me, Grandma," he said.

Staring at him as if she'd never seen him before, Grandma stood by the dressing table with a hairbrush in her hand.

“It’s only Arnold,” he said.

“Arnold!” she gasped. “Whatever were you doing under my bed?”

“I was thinking,” said Arnold.

The back door banged open.

"Mrs. Cline! Mrs. Cline!" Mr. Todd called out. "What's the matter?"

Grandma went out in the hall and called downstairs, "Oh, it's all right, Mr. Todd."

"I heard you scream. Are you sure you're all right?"

Charlie was barking like crazy.

"Everything's perfectly all right, Mr. Todd. Thank you. It was only Arnold. I— He scared me nearly to death. But it's all right now. Would you let Charlie in the house, please?"

Arnold put his arms around his grandmother. “I didn't mean to scare you, Grandma,” he said. “I'm sorry.”

And that was almost the truth.